Wiggle Waggle Fun

stories and rhymes for the very very young

Margaret Mayo

ALFRED A. KNOPF · NEW YORK

For my granddaughter Anna
and Francesca Dow's son Benedict
and with special thanks
to their big brothers
Jack and Lucian.
MM

THIS IS A BORZOI BOOK PUBLISHED BY ALFRED A. KNOPF

Text on pages 9, 10, 11, 12, 13, 16, 17, 18, 19, 24, 25, 26, 27, 28, 29, 30, 31, 33, 34, 35,
36, 37, 38, 39, 40, 42, 43, 44, 45, 46, 47, 48, 50, 51, 62, 63 copyright © 2000 by Margaret Mayo.
The illustrator acknowledgments on pages 4 and 5 constitute an extension of this copyright page.
Illustrations copyright © 2000 by the individuals credited.

www.randomhouse.com/kids

Library of Congress Cataloging-in-Publication Data
Plum pudding
Wiggle waggle fun : stories and rhymes for the very very young / [collected by] Margaret Mayo.
p.   cm.
Summary: A collection of poems, stories, traditional verses, action rhymes, and stories, illustrated by twenty-four different artists.
ISBN 0-375-81529-5 (trade) — ISBN 0-375-91529-X (lib. bdg.)
1. Children's literature. [1. Literature—Collections.] I. Mayo, Margaret. II. Title.
PZ5.P73 2002
808.8'9282—dc21
2001029568

First Borzoi Books edition: February 2002
Printed in Hong Kong
10 9 8 7 6 5 4 3 2 1

Wiggle Waggle Fun

Contents

Puff-puff, Choo-choo! pictures by David Wojtowycz 6

Wiggle Waggle and Crocodile Snap pictures by Lindsey Gardiner 8

Speckledy Hen Bakes a Cake pictures by Patrice Aggs 10

Boom! Boom! Boom! Oomm-pah!-pah! pictures by Tony Ross 14

Playtime for Animal Babies pictures by Nicola Smee 16

Toot-toot! Train! pictures by Helen Stephens 18

Old Mother Turtle and Her Friends pictures by Britta Teckentrup 20

Splishy-Sploshy Wet Day pictures by Susan Rollings 24

We Do Like to Be Beside the Seaside pictures by Lydia Monks 26

Looking for Bugs and Creepy-Crawlies pictures by Lydia Monks 27

A Good Name for a Teddy Bear pictures by Emma Chichester Clark 28

Granddad's Shed pictures by Jane Simmons 32

Cheesy Macaroni pictures by Leonie Shearing 34

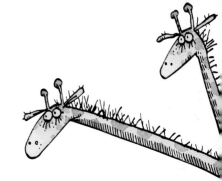

The Little House in the Woods pictures by Peter Bailey   36

Dig, Dig, Digging pictures by Alex Ayliffe   40

Favorite Pets pictures by Carol Thompson   42

Father Bear's Enormous Turnip pictures by Selina Young   44

A Boat Full of Animals pictures by Russell Ayto   48

Jack the Builder Man pictures by Sarah McConnell   50

It's Christmas Time! pictures by Karin Littlewood   52

Five Little Ducks pictures by Emily Bolam   54

Bathtime Fun pictures by Caroline Uff   58

Bedtime for Teddy Bear pictures by Caroline Uff   59

Hoddley, Poddley, Nonsense, and Fun pictures by Lauren Child   60

While You Are Sleeping pictures by Lisa Flather   62

Star Bright... pictures by Jane Ray   64

Puff-puff, Choo-choo!

Down at the station, early in the morning,
See the little puffer trains, all in a row.
See the engine driver pull a little handle,
Puff-puff, choo-choo, away we go!

Down at the garage, early in the morning,
See the little buses, all in a row.
See the bus driver pull a little handle,
Broom-broom, beep-beep, away we go!

Down at the farmyard, early in the morning,
See the little tractors, all in a row.
See the tractor driver pull a little handle,
Urr-urr, **chug-chug**, away we go!

Down at the fire station, early in the morning,
See the little fire engines, all in a row.
See the engine driver pull a little handle,
Nee-narr, **nee-narr**, away we go!

Wiggle Waggle and Crocodile Snap

Head, shoulders, knees and toes
Knees and toes
Head, shoulders, knees and toes
Knees and toes
Eyes and ears and mouth and nose
Head, shoulders, knees and toes
Knees and toes.

Waggle my fingers
And wriggle my toes,
Waggle my shoulders
And wiggle my nose.

Can you...

Snap like a crocodile

Curl up like a snail

Stretch out like a starfish

To the tips of your nails?

9

Speckledy Hen Bakes a Cake

Speckledy Hen and her five fluffy chicks lived in a little house with

Spotted Dog,

Ginger Cat, and

Pink Pig.

Speckledy Hen always did all the work, while Spotted Dog, Ginger Cat, and Pink Pig did none.

One day Speckledy Hen decided to bake a cake,
and she said, "Now who will help me mix the cake?"

"I won't," said Spotted Dog.
"I want to play."

"I won't," said
Ginger Cat.
"I want to play."

"And I won't,"
said Pink Pig. "I want to play too."

"Then I'll do it myself!" said Speckledy Hen.
So she mixed the butter, sugar, eggs, and flour, and her five fluffy chicks
gathered round, and they tried to help.

Cheep! cheep! cheep!

11

When the mixture was ready, Speckledy Hen called,
"Now who will help me cook the cake?"

"I won't," said Spotted Dog.
"I want to go for a run."

"I won't," said Ginger Cat.
"I want to climb a tree."

"And I won't," said Pink Pig.
"I want to go for a walk."

"Then I'll do it myself!" said Speckledy Hen.
And she poured the mixture into a tin, popped the tin in the hot oven,
and her five fluffy chicks gathered round, and they tried to help.

Cheep! cheep! cheep!

When the cake was cooked, Speckledy Hen took it out of the oven, and she called, "Now who will help me set the table?"

"I won't," said Spotted Dog. "I'm tired."

"I won't," said Ginger Cat. "I'm tired."

"And I won't," said Pink Pig. "I'm tired too."

"Then I'll do it myself!" said Speckledy Hen.

And she did, and her five fluffy chicks tried to help.

Cheep! cheep! cheep!

"Now," said Speckledy Hen, "who will help me EAT the cake?"

"I will!" cried Spotted Dog.

"I will!" cried Ginger Cat.

"And I will!" cried Pink Pig.

"Oh no, you won't!" said Speckledy Hen.

And she called her five fluffy chicks.

Then Speckledy Hen and her five fluffy chicks ate all the cake...

every

tiny

crumb!

BOOM! BOOM! BOOM!
OOMM - PAH! -PAH!

We can play on the big bass drum
And this is the way we do it:
BOOM! BOOM! BOOM!
Goes the big bass drum,
And that is the music to it.

We can play on the xylophone
And this is the way we do it:
PING! PONG! PONG!
Goes the xylophone,
And that is the music to it.

We can play on the silver flute
And this is the way we do it:
TOOT! TOOT! TOOT!
Goes the silver flute,
And that is the music to it.

We can play on the big fat tuba
And this is the way we do it:
OOMM-PAH!-PAH!
Goes the big fat tuba,
And that is the music to it.

We can play on the tambourine
And this is the way we do it:
JINGLY-JING!
Goes the tambourine,
And that is the music to it.

Playtime for Animal Babies

"Wake up, little monkey! Hold tight.
Away we go—swing-swing!
from tree to tree," says Monkey.

"Playtime, little cubs!
Let's rumble
and tumble . . . ,"
says Lion.

"Let's play roly-poly
in the soft snow, little bears,"
says Polar Bear.

"Sit on my back, little hippo.
I'm going for a swim,"
says Hippopotamus.

"Climb into my pocket,
little joey,"
says Kangaroo.
"Let's go for a bouncy ride."

"Time for a shower,
little calf,"
says Elephant.
"Swoosh!
sloosh!
sloosh!"

"Piggyback, little cub,"
says Koala.
"Up we go! Up, up, up!
High in the gum tree!"

"Cuddle up close, little chick,
and close your eyes,"
says Penguin.
"Sleepytime!"

Toot-toot! Train!

When Robbie goes to the park with Daddy and little Rachel,
they always walk down the road until they come to
the bridge over the railway tracks.

Then Robbie holds Daddy's hand, and they
climb the steps to the top of the bridge.

Robbie looks around. He waits and he listens.

At last he hears: ddd-dummm...ddd-dummm.

"Train!" shouts Robbie. And DDD-DUMM...

DDD-DUMM here comes the train rushing along the track,

DDD-DUMM... DDD-DUMM!

Robbie and Daddy wave. Little Rachel waves.

The train driver sounds his horn toot-toot! and waves back.

Whooo-oo! the train goes under the bridge and rushes on, right into a big tunnel.

"Bye-bye, train," says Robbie.

"Bye!" says little Rachel.

"Now," says Daddy, "let's go and play in the park." And off they go!

Old Mother Turtle
and Her Friends

1

Over in the meadow in the sand and the sun,
Lived Old Mother Turtle and her little turtle one.
"Dig," said his mother. "I dig," said the one.
So they dug all day in the sand and the sun.

2

Over in the meadow where the stream runs through,
Lived Old Mother Fish and her little fishes two.
"Swim," said their mother. "We swim," said the two.
So they swam all day where the stream runs through.

3

Over in the meadow in a hole in a tree,
Lived Old Mother Owl and her little owls three.
"Hoot," said their mother. "We hoot," said the three.
So they hooted all day in the hole in the tree.

4

Over in the meadow by the old barn door,
Lived Old Mother Mouse and her little mice four.
"Scamper," said their mother. "We scamper," said the four.
So they scampered all day by the old barn door.

5

Over in the meadow in a snug beehive,
Lived Old Mother Bee and her little bees five.
"Hum," said their mother. "We hum," said the five.
So they hummed all day round the snug beehive.

6

Over in the meadow in a nest built of sticks,
Lived Old Mother Crow and her little crows six.
"Caw," said their mother. "We caw," said the six.
So they cawed all day in the nest built of sticks.

7

Over in the meadow where the grass grows even,
Lived Old Mother Frog and her little frogs seven.
"Jump," said their mother. "We jump," said the seven.
So they jumped all day where the grass grows even.

8

Over in the meadow by the old wooden gate,
Lived Old Mother Squirrel and her little squirrels eight.
"Skip," said their mother. "We skip," said the eight.
So they skipped all day by the old wooden gate.

9

Over in the meadow near a tall dark pine,
Lived Old Mother Mole and her little moles nine.
"Burrow," said their mother. "We burrow," said the nine.
So they burrowed all day near the tall dark pine.

10 Over in the meadow in a muddy pigpen,
Lived Old Mother Pig and her little piglets ten.
"Squeal," said their mother. "We squeal," said the ten.
So they squealed all day in the muddy pigpen.

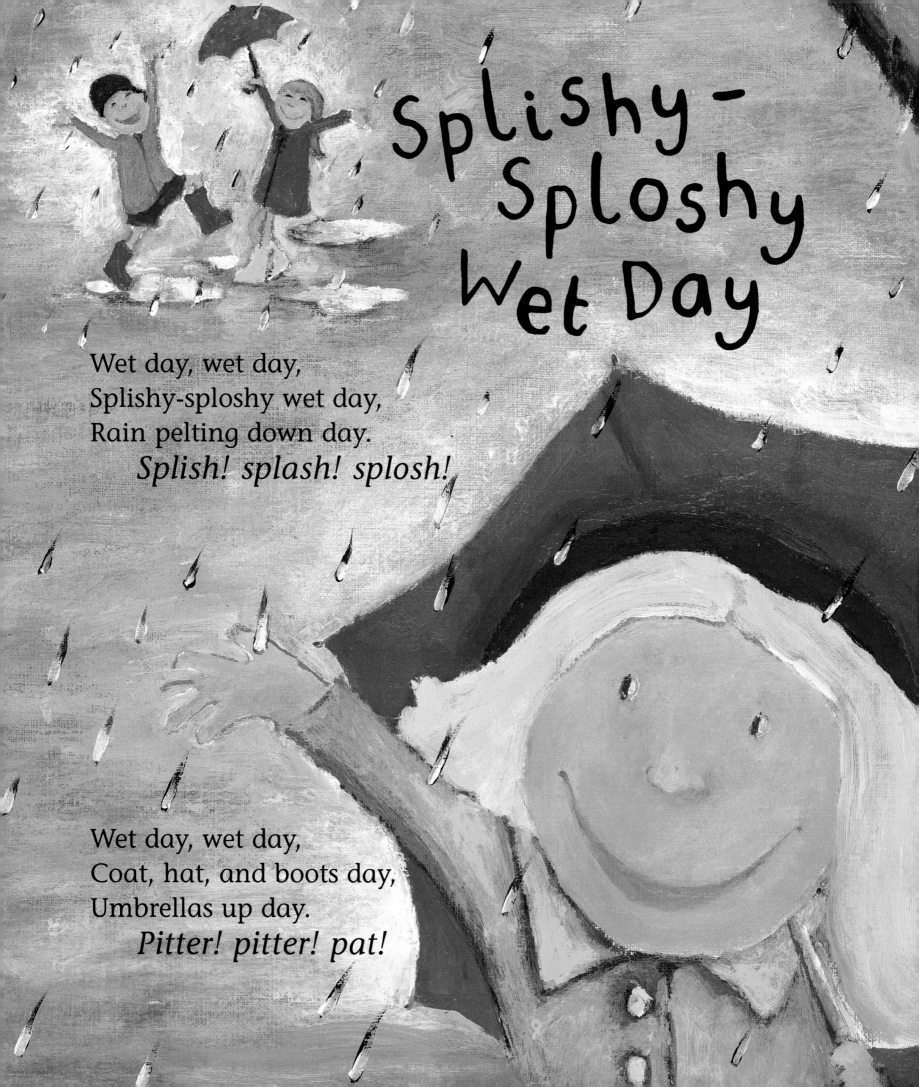

Splishy-Sploshy Wet Day

Wet day, wet day,
Splishy-sploshy wet day,
Rain pelting down day.
   Splish! splash! splosh!

Wet day, wet day,
Coat, hat, and boots day,
Umbrellas up day.
   Pitter! pitter! pat!

Wet day, wet day,
Cars swooshing by day,
Windshield wipers swishing day.
Swish! swish! swish!

Wet day, wet day,
Splishy-sploshy wet day,
Ducks love a wet day.
Do you?

We Do Like to Be Beside the Seaside

This little pig likes to build sand castles.

This little pig likes to sit in the sun.

This little pig likes to paddle and swim.

This little pig likes to splash his mum.

And this little pig likes to look for seashells, shiny stones, slippery seaweed, starfish, and lots and lots of special seaside things *and take them all home!*

Looking for Bugs and Creepy-Crawlies

1
One worm...
wriggle-wriggling.

2
Two spiders...
spin-spinning.

3
Three beetles...
crawl-crawling.

4
Four dragonflies...
dart-darting.

5
Five caterpillars...
nibble-nibbling.

6
Six butterflies...
flutter-fluttering.

7
Seven ladybugs...
shh...just resting.

8
Eight snails...
sliding and hiding.

9
Nine ants...
march-marching.

10
Ten bees...
buzz-buzz-buzzing

buzz

buzz

buzz!

A Good Name for a Teddy Bear

Anna's grandma gave her a lovely new teddy bear.
He had soft curly fur and a red ribbon tied round his neck.

"Thank you," said Anna.

"Now what will you call him?" said Grandma.

"I don't know," said Anna. "I'll go and ask my friends."

Anna skipped off and met
Brown Dog.

"What shall I call my teddy?"
asked Anna.

Brown Dog said, *"Woof! Woof!"*

"Woof?" said Anna. "That's *not*
a good name for a teddy bear!"

Anna skipped off and met Tabby Cat.

"What shall I call my teddy?" asked Anna.

Tabby Cat said, *"Mee-ow! Mee-ow!"*

"Mee-ow?" said Anna. "That's *not* a good name for a teddy bear!"

Anna skipped off and met Black Rooster.

"What shall I call my teddy?" asked Anna.

Black Rooster said, *"Cock-a-doodle-doo! Cock-a-doodle-doo!"*

"Cock-a-doodle-doo?" said Anna. "That's *not* a good name for a teddy bear!"

Anna skipped off and met Gray Donkey.

"What shall I call my teddy?" asked Anna.

Gray Donkey said, *"Heehaw! Heehaw!"*

"Heehaw?" said Anna. "That's *not* a good name for a teddy bear!"

Anna skipped off and met Green-headed Duck.

"What shall I call my teddy?" asked Anna.

Green-headed Duck said, *"Quack! Quack!"*

"Quack?" said Anna. "That's *not* a good name for a teddy bear!"

Anna skipped off and met Grandpa.

"What shall I call my teddy?" asked Anna.

Grandpa said, "You could call him Ted."

"Ted?" said Anna. "*Mmmm*…Ted's quite a good name…"

"He's a very cuddly teddy," said Grandpa.

"Cuddly Ted!" said Anna. "That's a *very* good name
for a teddy bear! I'll call him
Cuddly Ted!"

And she gave Cuddly Ted a big kiss on the nose.

Granddad's Shed

Granddad's shed is a special place.
I love to go in there,
And when I say, "Please, Granddad, please!"
He finds the key, unlocks the door,
And we step inside.

It's very, very dark,
But Granddad's there and I just love
To hold his hand and look around . . .

And stand and stare.

Cheesy Macaroni

(Sing to the tune of "Frère Jacques")

We like sausages! We like sausages!
Fish fingers too. How about you?
Spicy rice and noodles,
Cheesy macaroni,
Baked beans too. How about you?

We like carrots! We like carrots!
Potatoes too. How about you?
Aubergines and french beans,
Broccoli and green peas,
Sweet corn too. How about you?

We like bananas! We like bananas!
Strawberries too. How about you?
Pears and plums and peaches,
Kiwi fruit and melons,
Apples too. How about you?

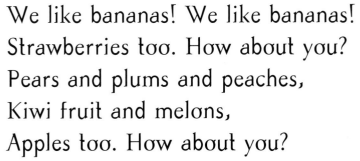

We like ice cream! We like ice cream!
Yogurt too. How about you?
Cherry pie and custard,
Chocolate cake and biscuits,
Cream buns too. How about you?

The Little House in the Woods

Early one morning Curly-tail Pig pushed open the gate of the pigpen and trotted off, *jiggety-jog!* to see his friend Woolly Sheep.

"Hello," said Woolly Sheep. "Where are you off to?"

Curly-tail Pig said, "I'm tired of living in a pigpen. So I'm going to build myself a little house in the woods."

"Oh, please, may I come with you?" said Woolly Sheep. "I could help! I could find logs and fix them in place."

"That's good!" said Curly-tail Pig. "Let's go!"

They trotted off, *jiggety-jog!* and they met White Goose.

"Hello," said White Goose. "Where are you off to?"

Curly-tail Pig said, "We're going to build ourselves a little house in the woods."

"Oh, please, may I come with you?" said White Goose. "I could help! I could find moss and stuff it in the holes to keep out the rain."

"That's good!" said Curly-tail Pig. "Let's go!"

They trotted off, *jiggety-jog!* and they met Cock Shiny-feathers.

"Hello," said Cock Shiny-feathers. "Where are you off to?"

Curly-tail Pig said, "We're going to build ourselves a little house in the woods."

"Oh, please, may I come with you?" said Cock Shiny-feathers. "I could help! Every morning, bright and early, I could crow— *cock-a-doodle-doo!*—and wake you up."

"That's good!" said Curly-tail Pig. "Let's go!"

They trotted off, *jiggety-jog!* until they came to a grassy place hidden in the woods.

"This is a good place to build our house," said Curly-tail Pig.

Then Curly-tail Pig and Woolly Sheep found logs and fixed them one on top of the other. White Goose found moss and stuffed it in the holes with her bill. And every morning, bright and early, Cock Shiny-feathers crowed— *cock-a-doodle-doo!*— and woke the others.

At last the walls were up, the roof was on, all the holes were filled, and their snug little house was built.

From then on Curly-tail Pig, Woolly Sheep, White Goose, and Cock Shiny-feathers lived happily together in their little house in the woods. They didn't quarrel except...sometimes...

when Cock Shiny-feathers
woke the others much too bright and early
in the morning with his loud cock-a-doodle-doo!

Dig, Dig, Digging

Dig, dig, digging,
Diggers are good at dig, dig, digging—
They can work all day.

Pull, pull, pulling,
Tractors are good at pull, pull, pulling—
They can work all day.

Lift, lift, lifting,
Cranes are good at lift, lift, lifting—
They can work all day.

Favorite Pets

Chloe has a cat
Mee-ow!

and Robert has a rabbit.
Snuffle! Snuffle!

Danny has a dog
Woof! Woof!

and Granny has a parrot.
Pretty Polly!

But Jess has a bear, a lion, a giraffe, a sheep, and
a hippopotamus. They are always very quiet.
They do everything Jess tells them to do.
And they sleep in Jess's bed every night.

Lucky Jess!

Father Bear's Enormous Turnip

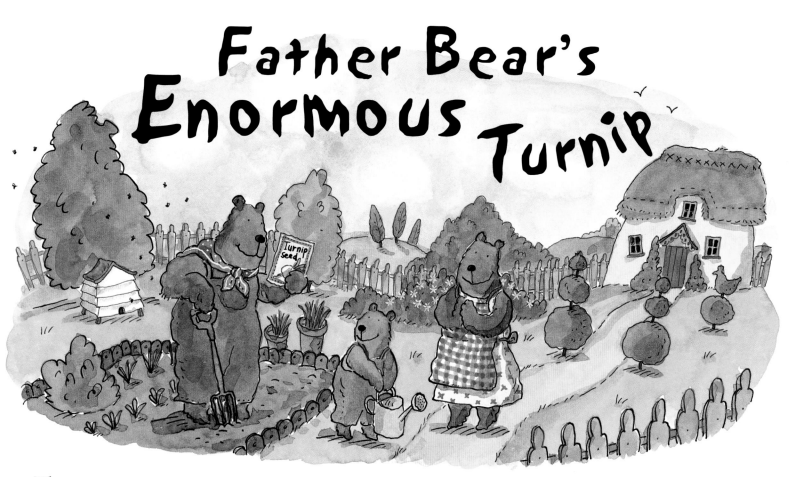

Father Bear, Mother Bear, and Little Bear lived in a house with a lovely garden all around.

One day Father Bear found a seed packet with a tiny turnip seed inside, and he planted the seed in his garden.
He said, "Grow, tiny seed! Grow!"

Before long a green shoot sprouted up, and then that turnip grew and it grew, and it GREW and it GREW until it was ENORMOUS.

Father Bear said, "That turnip is quite big enough. I must pull it up!"
So he took hold of the turnip,
and he pulled
and he pulled…
but he couldn't pull up the turnip.

Father Bear called Mother Bear, "Come and help!"

Pull … pull … pull!

Pull...pull...pull!

So Mother Bear pulled Father Bear, and Father Bear pulled the turnip.
They pulled
and they pulled...
but they couldn't pull up the turnip.
Mother Bear called Little Bear, "Come and help!"
So Little Bear pulled Mother Bear, Mother Bear pulled Father Bear, and

Father Bear pulled the turnip.
They pulled
and they pulled...
but they couldn't pull up the turnip.
Little Bear called Bushy-tail Squirrel, "Come and help!"
So Bushy-tail Squirrel pulled Little Bear, Little Bear pulled Mother Bear, Mother Bear pulled Father Bear, and Father Bear pulled the turnip.
They pulled
and they pulled
and they pulled...
but they couldn't pull up the turnip.
Bushy-tail Squirrel called Mouse Twitchy-whiskers, "Come and help!"

Pull....pull....pull!

So Mouse Twitchy-whiskers pulled
Bushy-tail Squirrel, Bushy-tail Squirrel pulled
Little Bear, Little Bear pulled Mother Bear,
Mother Bear pulled Father Bear, and
Father Bear pulled the turnip.
  They pulled
      and they pulled
          and they pulled…
but they couldn't pull up
the turnip.
  Mouse Twitchy-whiskers
called Teeny-weeny
Black Beetle,
"Come and help!"
  So Teeny-weeny
Black Beetle
pulled Mouse
Twitchy-whiskers,
Mouse Twitchy-whiskers pulled Bushy-tail Squirrel, Bushy-tail Squirrel
pulled Little Bear, Little Bear pulled Mother Bear, Mother Bear pulled
Father Bear, and Father Bear pulled the turnip.

Pull…pull…pull!

They pulled and

      they pulled

          and they pulled…

              and

whoo-oomp!…

UP CAME THE TURNIP!

And they all fell down in a tangly heap with the enormous turnip on top.

"Thanks for your help," said Father Bear.

"Now you must stay for supper," said Mother Bear.

Then she cooked a big pot of turnip stew, and everyone sat down to eat. They *were* hungry after all that pulling.

And that turnip stew was *delicious!*

47

A Boat Full of Animals

See the animals in the boat,
Two of everything all afloat.

Look, can you find them — two by two —
Two rhinoceroses, two kangaroos?

Two stripey zebras and two brown hares,
Penguins and parrots and grizzly bears.

Two snappy crocodiles, two big dogs,
Monkeys, elephants, and croaking frogs.

Long-necked giraffes, two tigers that growl.
Lions and raccoons and round-eyed owls.

Flamingos, doves, and snakes by the door.
Now, look again, can you see any more?

Jack the Builder Man

Here is Jack the builder man—
  and this is the house
    that Jack built.

Here are the bricks,
  the wood, and a heap of things—
    for building the house
      that Jack built.

Here are the chairs and table,
beds and cot, television, toys,
and a muddle of things—
  moving into the house
    that Jack built.

Here are the rooms with chairs
and table, beds and cot,
television, toys,
and that muddle of things—
all nicely arranged
inside the house
that Jack built.

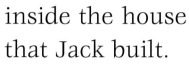

Here are the people—Emma and Tom,
their mum and their dad,
their dog and their cat—
who now live
in the house
that Jack built.

It's Christmas Time!

The north wind doth blow
And we shall have snow,
And what will poor robin do then,
    Poor thing?
He'll sit in a barn,
And keep himself warm,
And hide his head under his wing,
    Poor thing!

Jingle bells, jingle bells,
Jingle all the way;
Here comes Santa riding by
With his reindeer and his sleigh.

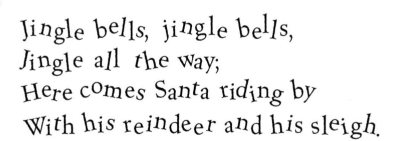

Away in a manger, no crib for a bed,
The little Lord Jesus laid down his sweet head.
The stars in the bright sky looked down where he lay,
The little Lord Jesus asleep on the hay.

The cattle are lowing, the baby awakes,
But the little Lord Jesus no crying he makes.
I love thee, Lord Jesus! Look down from the sky
And stay by my bedside till morning is nigh.

Five Little Ducks

Five little ducks went swimming one day,
Over the hills and far away.

Mother Duck said, "Quack, quack, quack, quack."
But only four little ducks came back.

Four little ducks went swimming one day,
Over the hills and far away.

Mother Duck said, "Quack, quack, quack, quack."
But only three little ducks came back.

Three little ducks went swimming one day,
Over the hills and far away.
Mother Duck said, "Quack, quack, quack, quack."
But only two little ducks came back.

Two little ducks went swimming one day,
Over the hills and far away.
Mother Duck said, "Quack, quack, quack, quack."
But only one little duck came back.

One little duck went swimming one day,
Over the hills and far away.
Mother Duck said, "QUACK, QUACK, QUACK, QUACK!"

And ALL her five little ducks came back!

Bathtime Fun

The big ship sails on the alley alley oh,
The alley alley oh, the alley alley oh;
The big ship sails on the alley alley oh,
On the last day of September.

The yellow duck floats on the alley alley oh,
The alley alley oh, the alley alley oh;
The yellow duck floats on the alley alley oh,
On the last day of September.

We all scrub-a-dub in the alley alley oh,
The alley alley oh, the alley alley oh;
We all scrub-a-dub in the alley alley oh,
On the last day of September.

Bedtime for Teddy Bear

Teddy bear,
Teddy bear,
Turn around.
Teddy bear,
Teddy bear,
Touch the ground.

Teddy bear,
Teddy bear,
Peek-a-boo!
Teddy bear,
Teddy bear—
Now skiddoo!

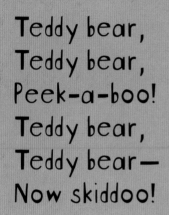

Teddy bear,
Teddy bear,
Climb the stairs.
Teddy bear,
Teddy bear,
Say your
prayers.

Teddy bear,
Teddy bear,
Turn out the light.
Teddy bear,
Teddy bear,
Say good night!

Hoddley, Poddley, Nonsense, and Fun

Hoddley, poddley, puddles, and frogs,
Cats are to marry the poodle dogs:
Cats in blue jackets and dogs in red hats,
What will become of the mice and the rats?

Yankee Doodle came to town
Riding on a pony:
Stuck a feather in his hat
And called it macaroni!

I asked my mother for fifty cents
To see the elephant jump the fence.
He jumped so high,
He reached the sky.
He never came back
Till the Fourth of July!

Diddle, diddle, dumpling, my son John,
Went to bed with his trousers on:
One shoe off, and one shoe on,
Diddle, diddle, dumpling, my son John.

Three little ghosties
Sitting on posties,
Eating buttered toasties,
Greasy fisties,
Up to their wristies.
Oh, what beasties:
Such messy feasties!

While You Are Sleeping

When night has come
And it is dark,

Bats swoop,

Owls hoot,

Snails creep,

Cats prowl,

Foxes bark,

Frogs croak,

Hedgehogs snuffle.

62

While warm and safe
In your own little bed,
   you close your eyes
   and sleep.

Good night . . . good night!

Star Bright...

Star light, star bright,
First star I see tonight,
I wish I may, I wish I might,
Have the wish, I wish tonight.

The stars shine bright,
The moon gives light,
So—a big kiss
For everyone
And say, "Good night!"